Undersea City

A Story of a Caribbean Coral Reef

For Honey, who would have loved a book about fish. — D.M.R.

To Heidi and Clay — K.L.

Book design: Shields & Partners, Westport, CT

First Edition 1997
10 9 8 7 6 5 4 3 2
Printed in China

Acknowledgements:
   Our very special thanks to the staffs of The Nature Conservancy in Arlington, Virginia, and the Marine Conservation Science Center in Miami, Florida, for their review and guidance.

Library of Congress Cataloging-in-Publication Data

Rau, Dana Meachen, 1971-

Undersea city: a story of a Caribbean coral reef / by Dana Meachen Rau ; illustrated by Katie Lee.
         p.   cm.
Summary: A hermit crab searching for a new shell is carried by a wave from the shore to a coral reef, where he encounters many different kinds of creatures before trying to make his way back to the shore.
         ISBN 1-56899-433-8 (hardcover)   ISBN 1-56899-434-6 (pbk.)
1. Hermit crabs — Juvenile fiction. [1. Hermit crabs — Fiction. 2. Crabs — Fiction. 3. Coral reef animals — Fiction. 4. Coral reefs and islands — Fiction.]
I. Lee, Katie, 1942- ill. II. Title.
         PZ10.3.R185Un 1997   96-39099
         [Fic] — dc21   CIP
                                                                AC

Undersea City

**A Story of
a Caribbean
Coral Reef**

by Dana Meachen Rau
illustrated by Katie Lee

™ **Sound**prints
Where Children Discover...

The beach is dotted with shells, washed in by the breaking waves. On Saona Island, off the coast of the Dominican Republic, the shells glisten in the moonlight like jewels from a lost treasure. Snails once lived in these periwinkle shells, tulip shells, moon shells, and whelks. But now they lie empty.

Nearby, in a red mangrove tree, a land hermit crab nibbles the leaves. Part of his body is curled into a moon shell, which he wears for protection. He ambles along the long mangrove roots that hang down into the salty ocean water. The mangrove shelters the island coast and the young damselfish and barracudas that feed on the growing seaweed in the water below.

4

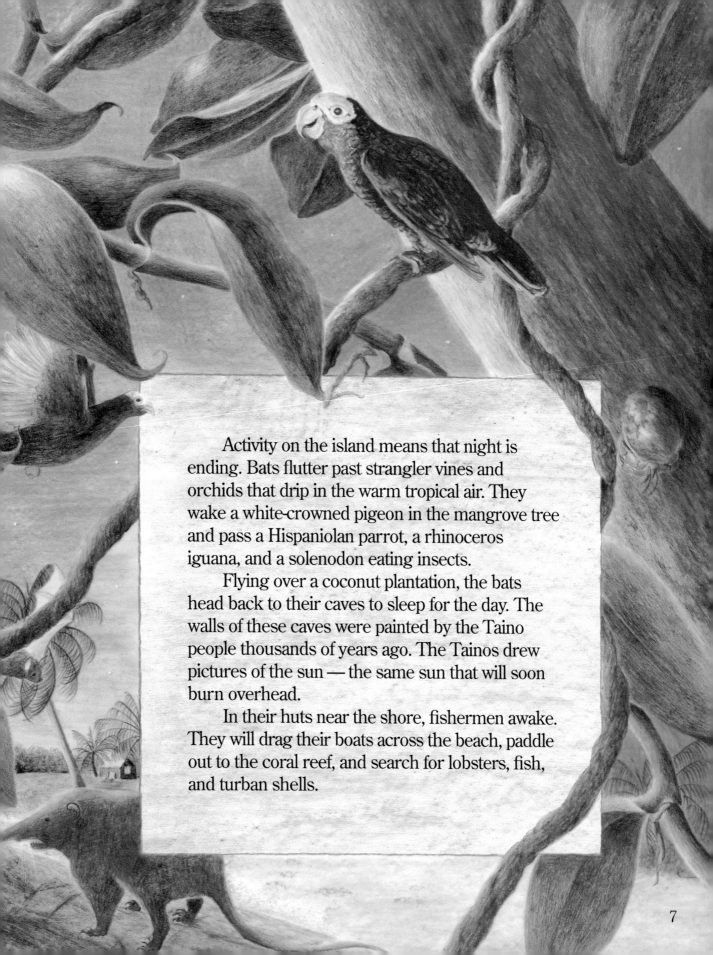

Activity on the island means that night is ending. Bats flutter past strangler vines and orchids that drip in the warm tropical air. They wake a white-crowned pigeon in the mangrove tree and pass a Hispaniolan parrot, a rhinoceros iguana, and a solenodon eating insects.

Flying over a coconut plantation, the bats head back to their caves to sleep for the day. The walls of these caves were painted by the Taino people thousands of years ago. The Tainos drew pictures of the sun — the same sun that will soon burn overhead.

In their huts near the shore, fishermen awake. They will drag their boats across the beach, paddle out to the coral reef, and search for lobsters, fish, and turban shells.

While the fishermen prepare their nets, the hermit crab crawls onto the sandy beach and pokes at a few shells with his claws. He is growing larger, and his shell is getting cramped. The moon shell is a good home, but it will soon be too small. He must find a new one.

A turban shell would be perfect, but they are rare. Fishermen have hunted most of the turban shell snails.

At the edge of the water lies a tulip shell. The hermit crab picks it up to test its weight. The opening seems large enough. Uncurling his body from the moon shell, he sticks it into the new one. Too tight! He curls back into his old shell.

Suddenly, WHOOSH! A wave whips him off the sand, and a strong current carries him out toward the open sea.

The choppy waves spin him in circles and drop him onto the coral reef, far from shore. Right away, he starts back toward the beach. He cannot survive underwater for long.

Luckily, morning is approaching as the hermit crab crawls across the reef. The dangerous hunters of the night are leaving. A crowd of jacks whizzes past like a lightning flash. A shark snatches one last fish and heads out to sea. Pilot fish follow, hoping to get a scrap of the shark's meal.

The coral looks like a flower garden. Thousands of tiny coral polyps poke out of their limestone cups. Years and years of old polyps have left empty cups behind. They have piled up to make the lumpy, bumpy coral reef.

Spiky sea urchins drag themselves across the ocean floor. Brittle stars glow in the dark to scare away enemies. The reef is like a city, filled with action.

The hermit crab waddles toward the shore. As the sun's first rays break through the water, the coral polyps pull themselves into their cups. Now, instead of a garden, the coral looks like stone.

Some fishes' scales change to match the colors of the sunlit reef. A blue tang turns brighter blue, and a red squirrelfish turns brighter red. Now it will be hard for enemies to see them.

Among the sea fans, the striped drums make their thumping sound to greet the morning. Daytime fish of all colors and patterns come out from holes in the reef and bustle around the coral city on their morning errands. Most stop for food. Some stop for a cleaning.

Near the brain coral, the bold stripes of the gobies have attracted a line of larger fish. Boxfish and groupers patiently wait their turn to be cleaned. Here at the cleaning station, the crew of gobies works nonstop.

They nibble parasites from a boxfish's scales. When they are done, the boxfish swims off, and they work on the next fish in line.

The hermit crab crosses a pile of rocks as the boxfish and groupers swarm above him. Just ahead, he spots the perfect new home — a turban shell! But when he pokes the shell, it moves! The snail inside thrusts forward across the sea floor on its large snail foot.

A shadow creeps over the coral. The hermit crab hides, just like he does on the beach when a seagull flies too close. He pulls his legs into his shell and blocks the entrance with his larger claw. It is a ray, soaring through the water like a bird through the sky. It isn't interested in the hermit crab and slips away.

The hermit crab ventures through a patch of turtle grass. He crawls past a trumpetfish hiding. Its long thin body sways with the grass, waiting for an unsuspecting fish to wander past. A manatee swims through the seagrass, too.

The hermit crab is getting tired. He passes another patch of coral. This part of the reef is new. It has finally grown back after an anchor ripped through the coral many years ago.

Sponges on the coral suck in water, like vacuum cleaners. Munching and crunching, a striped parrotfish snacks on the coral.

When a foureye butterflyfish swims by, a moray eel pops out of a crack in the coral like a jack-in-the-box. The fish should be an easy catch for the eel, because it looks like it is swimming right toward him. But the fish has black spots that look like eyes on the back of its body. It darts away in the other direction!

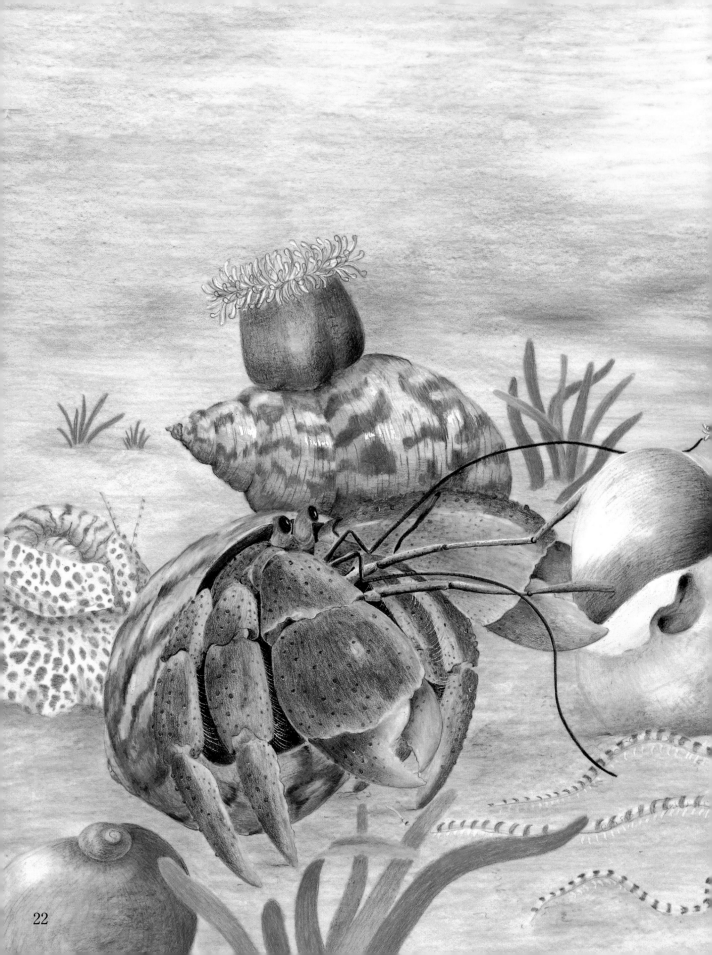

Growing weaker, the hermit crab scurries over to a pile of shells. Snails are still inside some.

One empty shell is covered with sea anemones. All the fish avoid the anemones' sting.

But the hermit crab is safe. His body armor protects him. He picks up the empty shell with one claw to see if it would be a good fit.

A sea star approaches! The crab snaps at it with his other claw. Still, it creeps closer.

Then, one of the sea star's five legs brushes the sea anemone. The sea star coils back from the sting and slinks away as fast as it can.

There is no time to try the shell now. The hermit crab scuttles toward shore. It is already mid-morning, and the trip back is too far. He can't survive much longer.

He stops to rest in some sea grass. A net sweeps by, scooping up hundreds of fish in its path. The netting wraps around the hermit crab's claws! Soon, he is bobbing at the surface of the water in a tangle of string. Fishermen hoist the net into their boat.

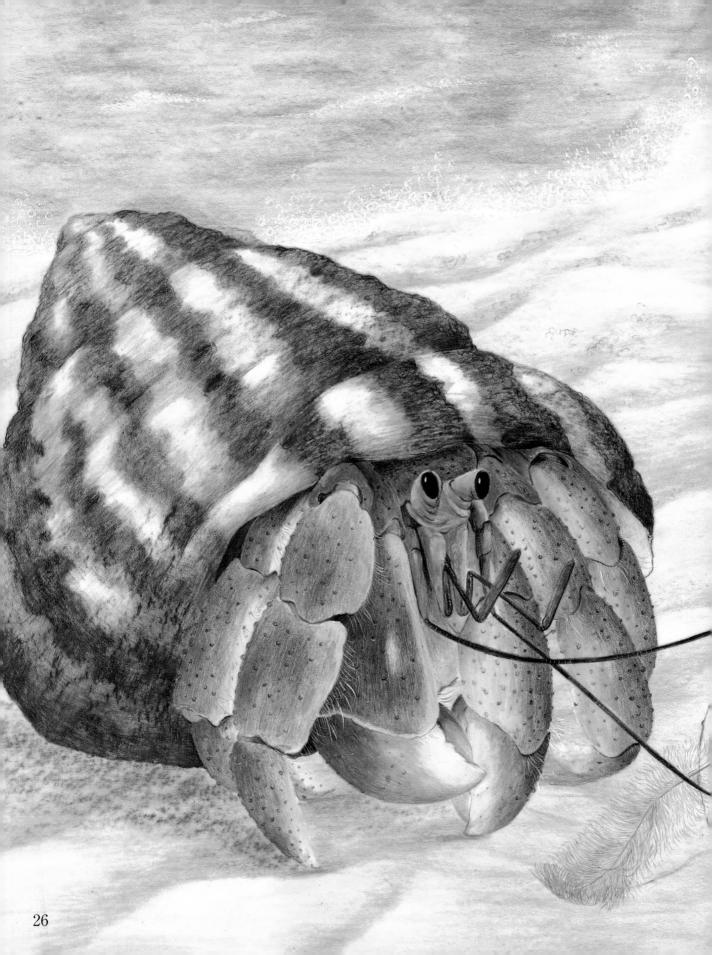

When the fishermen reach the shore, they unload their nets, and carry them across the sand. The hermit crab and other shells fall out and roll onto the beach. The hermit crab pulls himself into his home until the fishermen have gone and the coast is clear.

Slowly, he peeks out. Before him, large and white with brown-striped spirals, is a turban shell!

He inspects it, poking his head into the swirled pearly pink inside. He rolls it and rocks it and cleans out the sand. Then, slipping out of his old shell, he slides into the turban shell. It is a perfect fit — a gift from the coral reef.

Saona Island

Land hermit crabs can be found on Saona Island, a small Caribbean island south of the Dominican Republic. Saona Island is home to many species of plants and animals that can only be found in the Dominican Republic.

About Saona Island

Saona Island, off the coast of the Dominican Republic, is the site of the coral reef in this story. Like other coral reef habitats throughout the world, the Saona Island reef provides food and shelter for many kinds of fish, birds, crabs, shrimp, sponges, sea urchins, and even some mammals, such as dolphins and manatees.

Corals are composed of tiny sea animals, called polyps that make up the reef itself. They need warm, shallow, tropical or subtropical water to grow. When a polyp dies, it leaves its limestone skeleton behind. As new polyps grow on top of this foundation, the coral reef is formed. It takes thousands of years for a reef to grow.

The animals of the coral reef depend on each other and the reef for survival. The lives of the plants and animals of the reef are so connected that if anything changes, such as an anchor destroying a piece of the reef, the whole habitat must adjust to the change.

Land hermit crabs live in and around the mangrove trees on Saona Island's shores. During the day, they hide under leaves or other cover, and at night they scavenge for food. Land hermit crabs live only on tropical and subtropical coasts where the temperature is warm and the air is wet. Because they do not have strong outer shells over their entire bodies like other crabs, they must borrow abandoned shells from dead sea snails to use as shelter.

The Taino people lived on Saona Island thousands of years ago. Today, about five hundred people live there. Scientists are watching the island and waters that surround it very closely to be sure it stays healthy. Agriculture, deforestation, hunting, over fishing, and tourism threaten the island and the reef, and may lead to the disappearance or extinction of plants and animals that are found on Saona Island.

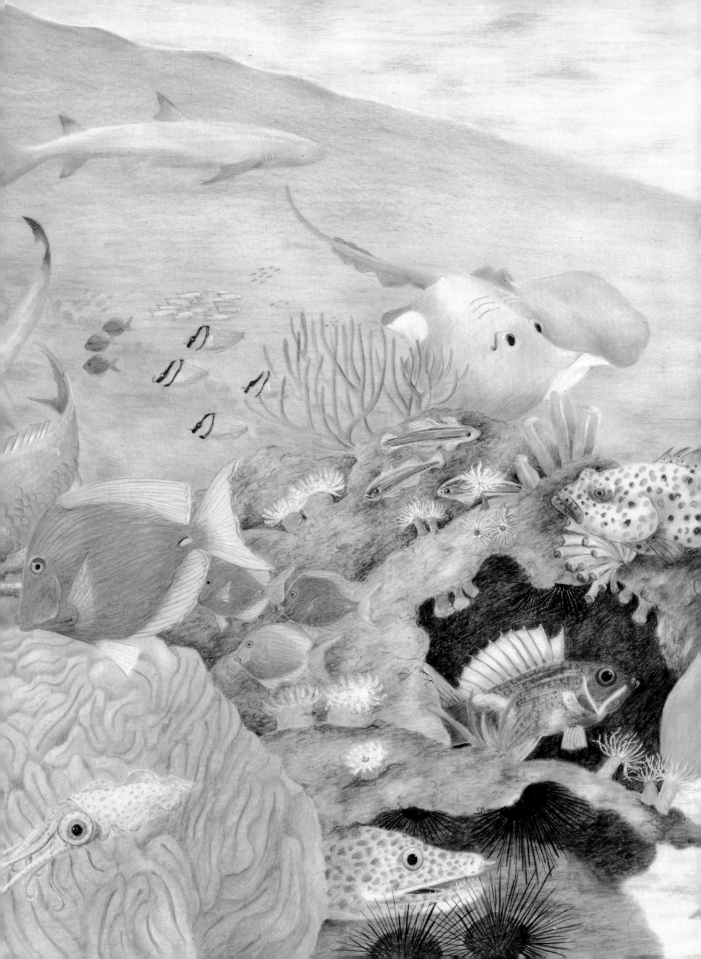

Glossary

 Colorful
Atlantic
Natica

 Land
Hermit
Crab

 Scrawled
Cowfish
(Boxfish)

 Cushion
Sea Star

 Manatee

 Solenodon

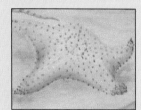 Dwarf
Brown
Periwinkle

 Prickly
Periwinkle

 Strangler
Vine

 Fishing
Bat

 Red
Mangrove

 Turtle
Grass

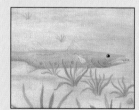 Great
Barracuda

 Rhinoceros
Iguana

 Vanilla
Orchid

 Hispaniolan
Parrot

 Sand
Drum

 White
Crowned
Pigeon

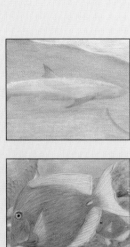 *Blacktip Shark*

 *Long-spined Black Urchin*

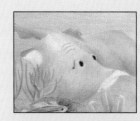 *Southern Stingray*

 *Blue Tang*

 *Neon Goby*

 *Spotted Moray Eel*

 *Depressed Brain Coral*

 *Pilot Fish*

 *Squirrelfish*

 *Foureye Butterflyfish*

 *Queen Parrotfish*

 *Trumpet Fish*

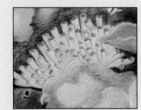 *Giant Caribbean Anemone*

 *Red Hind Grouper*

 *Yellow Boring Sponge*

 *Bar Jack*

 *Sea Fan*

 *Yellowtail Damselfish*